# DOLLY PARTON
## COUNTRY GOIN' TO TOWN

BY SUSAN SAUNDERS

Illustrated by Rodney Pate

PUFFIN BOOKS

*For Margaret Albrecht, an excellent teacher*

PUFFIN BOOKS

Viking Penguin Inc., 40 West 23rd Street, New York, New York 10010, U.S.A.
Penguin Books Ltd, Harmondsworth, Middlesex, England
Penguin Books Australia Ltd, Ringwood, Victoria, Australia
Penguin Books Canada Limited, 2801 John Street, Markham, Ontario, Canada L3R 1B4
Penguin Books (N.Z.) Ltd, 182–190 Wairau Road, Auckland 10, New Zealand

First published by Viking Penguin Inc. 1985
Published in Puffin Books 1986
3  5  7  9  10  8  6  4  2
Text copyright © Susan Saunders, 1985
Illustrations copyright © Rodney Pate, 1985
All rights reserved
Printed in U.S.A. by R. R. Donnelley & Sons Company, Harrisonburg, Virginia
Set in Garamond #3

*Women of Our Time* ® is a registered trademark of Viking Penguin Inc.

Grateful acknowledgment is made to the following for permission to reprint copyrighted material:
*Tree Publishing Co., Inc.:* Portions of lyrics from "Dumb Blonde," by Curly Putman.
Copyright © 1966 Tree Publishing Co., Inc. International copyright secured.
All rights reserved. Used by permission of the publisher.
*Velvet Apple Music:* Portions of lyrics from "Coat of Many Colors," by Dolly Parton.
© 1969 Velvet Apple Music (BMI). From "In the Good Old Days (When Times Were Bad),"
by Dolly Parton. © 1968 Velvet Apple Music (BMI).
All rights reserved. Used by permission.

Library of Congress Cataloging in Publication Data
Saunders, Susan.     Dolly Parton, country goin' to town.
Reprint. Originally published: New York: Viking, 1985.
Summary: A biography of the singer and writer of country music, with emphasis
on her childhood and youth.
1. Parton, Dolly—Juvenile literature.   2. Country musician—United States—Biography—Juvenile
literature.   [1. Parton, Dolly.   2. Musicians]   1. Pate, Rodney, ill.   II. Title.
[ML3930.P25S3  1986]     784.5'2'00924   [B]   [92]     86-3239     ISBN 0-14-032162-4

# CONTENTS

# DOLLY PARTON
## COUNTRY GOIN' TO TOWN

# 1

# Smoky Mountain Roots

As a little girl, Dolly Parton loved to sing. And she had a big imagination. When her older brothers and sister were at school and she no longer had a real audience, she climbed a tree in back of the house. From her perch, she pretended that she was on stage. Stretched out in front of her was an imaginary audience of thousands of people, all there waiting to hear her.

Now it is hard to imagine anyone who *hasn't* heard Dolly Parton. She is a singer who has sold millions of records. She is a songwriter who has published more than three thousand songs. She has had her own television show, has starred in TV specials and in movies. She is a businesswoman who owns her own music publishing company, real estate, and a film production company.

Where did it all start? It began in an old log cabin down in a "holler" in the Great Smoky Mountains.

The Great Smokies sprawl across the border between Tennessee and North Carolina. They are among the oldest mountains in the world. And they are beautiful, covered with hardwood forests, threaded with streams. They were first settled centuries ago by Cherokee Indians.

The Cherokees hunted the game that roamed the woods. They fished for trout in the streams. They had raspberries, blueberries, walnuts, and hickories for the picking.

Then, around 1800, European pioneers came over the mountains. Scottish, Irish, English, they followed old Indian trails into the Smokies. They built their log cabins down in the "hollers"—hollows, little valleys among the hills and ridges—out of the way of the winds and storms that swept across the mountains. With them they brought cows, pigs, and chickens. And they farmed, planting corn and turnips, potatoes and beans. Their farms and villages were so cut off from the outside world that their way of life changed little from that time to this.

"We made our own soap, ground our own meal.

About all we had to buy was coffee, sugar, and flour. We were hungry for a variety of things. But as far as going hungry with our bellies empty, we never had to do that." Those words could have been spoken by one of the early pioneers. But in fact, they're the words of Dolly Parton. She's talking about how things were in the mountains not long ago, in the 1950s, when she was a little girl.

Dolly was born on January 19, 1946, in a pine-log cabin at the end of a rutted trail in Sevier County, Tennessee. The doctor who delivered her rode into the snowy hollow on a horse. Dolly's father didn't have the money to pay him for his visit. So he paid the doctor with a sack of the family's corn meal.

Dolly's older sister, Willadeene, says, "She was the most beautiful baby . . . the first in our family with blond hair and fair, ivory skin."

Dolly looked like her father, Lee Parton, who was blond and Scotch-Irish. Dolly's mother, Avie Lee Owens Parton, was one-quarter Cherokee Indian. And she had the black hair to prove it.

Avie Lee married Lee Parton when she was fifteen, he seventeen. They had their first child, Willadeene, less than a year later. Next came David, and after him, Denver. And then Dolly. The Partons were to have eight more children after Dolly: Bobby, Stella, Cassie, Randy, Larry, the twins, Floyd and Frieda, and last, Rachel. There were twelve in all, six girls and six boys.

But one of the boys, Larry, lived for only a few hours after he was born.

Although the Partons weren't the poorest people in Sevier County, not many had less. Dolly's father worked hard to support his family, growing vegetables to eat and tobacco to sell. He also took jobs as a construction worker, digging ditches in Knoxville, forty miles away, to make extra money.

Even so, as Dolly explains it, the Partons hit some "rough spots." There were times when they couldn't afford to pay the rent where they were living and had to find a cheaper place. They moved often, from one worn-out farm to another, from one weathered shack to the next.

Dolly jokes about it now: "Most people have three rooms and a bath. We had four rooms and a path." What she means is there was no indoor plumbing, no running water—all their water had to be brought from a well outside—and for a time, no electricity. They were crowded, the children sleeping as many as four or five to a bed. And often they were cold.

Dolly would write a song about it later called "In the Good Old Days (When Times Were Bad)":

> *We've got up before*
> *And found ice on the floor*
> *Where the wind would blow snow*
> *Through cracks in the wall.*

But there were good times, too. As Dolly has said, "We had absolutely nothin'. But we did have a lot of love and fun." At night, Avie Lee told the children tall tales and scary ghost stories—as Dolly points out, what better way to get all those children to go to bed and *stay* there?

And there was singing. Avie Lee had a good voice. She knew the words to many of the old folk ballads sung in the Smokies. Dolly's father played the guitar and banjo. And the children sang along. Her mother remembers Dolly could carry a tune before she learned to talk.

The Partons had no car. For them, like many other mountain families, church was the center of their social life. And they walked to the small church down the road, not only on Sundays, but often three or four times a week. There were evening services, prayer meetings, and revivals—enthusiastic renewals of faith—that sometimes went on for days.

Dolly's grandfather Jake Owens was the preacher. And, as Dolly remembers it, many of the services were "mostly music." First the congregation would listen to a scorching sermon. Then they were encouraged to "shout out," to "make a joyful noise unto the Lord," and they did. To the accompaniment of fiddles, guitars, tambourines, and banjos, they would sing any song they particularly liked, as well as hymns and spirituals. It was there that Dolly first sang in public.

And it was in her grandfather's church that she learned to find lifelong guidance and comfort in the Bible.

"You have to go by Scripture," Dolly says now. Her strength, she came to believe, was from God.

When Dolly started going to school, she went to a one-room schoolhouse called Mountain View. There were twenty-five children at Mountain View in grades one through seven. They walked two and a half miles up a dirt road to get to school. During the winter months, they would arrive half-frozen and have to huddle near the woodstove to thaw out a little. Then before classes started, there was a morning chapel service.

Dolly would get up in front of all the other children and sing the hymns she sang in church. Sometimes she sang some of the old Smoky Mountain folk songs Avie Lee had taught her.

Dolly had a remarkable memory, even as a small child. One of her teachers says she never forgot a single word of the long ballads she sang. The teacher also says that Dolly's memory was so good that she didn't have to work very hard in school. She could memorize a whole lesson the first time she heard it!

Another teacher recalls some other things about Dolly when she was small. "She could wink the keenest of any kid I ever saw," he says. And she liked to use the red crayons at school to color her lips and her cheeks. At seven, she was already fascinated with makeup.

Dolly herself describes the trouble she got into at home for wearing flour as powder and Mercurochrome as lipstick. The Mercurochrome stung her— and so did the spanking she got from her father. But Dolly was happy. Her lips were red. And it lasted for days!

The Parton children often helped their father in the fields. But while her brothers and sisters were gathering the potatoes the plow had turned up, Dolly was picking up shiny rocks and bits of glass. "I was

sure we had struck diamonds," she says. "I just loved the beauty of the things, the sparkle."

Her favorite fairy tales were those about kings and queens, with their fancy clothes and fabulous jewels. Dolly was beginning to dream of having such things herself some day.

# 2

# A Dreamer and a Doer

Dolly has said that being the fourth child in a large family was good for her. While attention was focused on those older or younger than she was, Dolly had time to think and to dream. But she also talks about being born in an "odd spot." She says she knows her parents "loved us all the same." But sometimes she felt she was being overlooked, lost in the crowd of brothers and sisters. Dolly says maybe it was because she *needed* to be special that she began to think she *was* special.

On Saturday nights, when she was supposed to be

asleep, Dolly would listen to the Grand Ole Opry. Even now the most famous country-music radio show, the Grand Ole Opry was beamed across the Smokies from Nashville.

The Opry had been on the air since the 1920s. In the beginning the performers were usually amateurs. They were people living in and around Nashville for whom music was a hobby, not a living. There were singers along with the banjo players, fiddlers, and guitar pickers. But the singers were no more important than anyone else in the bands.

By the time Dolly started to listen to the Grand Ole Opry, things had changed. Singers had become the stars of the four-and-a-half-hour show.

Her father's battery radio crackled with static. But Dolly could hear the kings and queens of country music singing live in front of a huge audience. Soon Dolly started telling people that someday *she* was going to sing at the Grand Ole Opry.

When she was six, Dolly had made a "guitar" for herself, from a broken mandolin and two bass guitar strings. The sounds that came out of it were droning and gloomy. But Dolly plucked at it faithfully and composed more songs. She had composed her first before she could write—her mother wrote the words down for her.

Dolly sang all the time: when she was washing dishes, on her way to school and back, when she helped put the younger children to bed. When she was eight years old, her uncle Bill Owens bought her a real guitar, a small Martin.

Bill Owens and two more of Avie Lee's brothers were musicians in a local band. Bill himself was a songwriter. Dolly says now, "My Uncle Bill was the one who saw so much in me."

Her sister Willadeene remembers that kids at school teased Dolly about her dreams of stardom. But Dolly had faith. One of her favorite passages in the Bible said, "If ye have faith as a grain of mustard seed . . . nothing shall be impossible unto you." Dolly truly believed she could do whatever she wanted, so their teasing didn't really hurt.

What did hurt, and hurt very badly, was the time they laughed at her coat. The fall Dolly was nine, she needed a new coat. Her mother, Avie Lee, made most of the clothes for the family. But that fall the Partons couldn't afford to buy the fabric for a coat.

Then Avie Lee remembered a box of scraps a neighbor had given her. Perhaps if she pieced them carefully together, she would have enough for a coat for her daughter.

Dolly cared very much about her appearance. So at first she wasn't sure about the coat her mother was sewing for her out of scraps of green, blue, and yellow corduroy—until Avie Lee told her the Bible story of Joseph, whose father had loved him so much that he made him a coat of many colors. Soon Dolly started feeling she was the luckiest girl in the mountains to have such a special coat made for her. She knew Avie Lee's love was sewed in every stitch.

Dolly was so proud of her new coat that she wore it to have her school picture taken. But some of her classmates snickered and teased. When Dolly tried to tell them how special the coat was, they laughed at how poor she must be to wear something made of scraps. They ended up locking her in the coat closet in the dark, until, Dolly says, she "went into a screaming fit."

When she told her mother about it, Avie Lee said,

"They're only looking with their eyes. You're looking with your heart." But for Dolly, it was, and is, one of the saddest, most painful things that happened in her life. Years later she turned it into a song called "Coat of Many Colors":

> I tried to make them see
> That one is only poor
> Only if they choose to be
> Now I knew we had no money
> But I was rich as I could be
> In my Coat of Many Colors
> My mama made for me.

If anything, Dolly became even more determined about her singing. When she became a star, she'd be able to buy all the clothes she wanted. "I was going to be rich," she says, "so I could buy things for Momma and Daddy, so I could buy them a big house, and we could have things."

She first sang on stage at the Paris Theater in nearby Sevierville. Cas Walker, a Knoxville businessman and politician, sponsored a live country and gospel radio show at the Paris on Saturday afternoons. One Saturday, Dolly volunteered to sing a gospel song. She was so scared that her knees were knocking together. But the audience loved her. And Dolly loved the applause.

Cas Walker had several weekly radio shows in

Knoxville, too. He invited Dolly to sing on them a few times over the next two years. Then, when Dolly was ten years old, he asked her to be a regular on the early-morning program—the *Farm and Home Hour*—and the noon show.

The *Farm Hour* was broadcast live at 5:30 in the morning. At 4 a.m. a friend or relative—usually Dolly's Aunt Estelle—would drive Dolly the forty miles from Sevierville to Knoxville to sing, then drive her back to school. Sometimes Dolly traveled back to Knoxville to sing on the noon show as well. She was paid twenty dollars a week.

Dolly could, Mr. Walker says, play a guitar and sing, or sing without a guitar. She could sing with a band, a quartet, or alone. She could sing country-and-western or gospel. He calls her a "miracle singer." He also says Dolly was "as independent as a hog on ice." Not yet a teenager, she didn't let anyone push her around. If the band musicians didn't play the way Dolly felt they should, she let them know about it. And if that didn't work, she took it up with the boss, Mr. Walker. As a friend said later, "Dolly knew from the first day she went into the business where she was going."

Dolly's voice was mature when she was eleven years old—a high, clear mountain soprano. Dolly herself matured early as well. When she was twelve, she looked much as she does now—blue-green eyes, almost perfect features, beautiful skin, and an hourglass figure. As Cas Walker says, when she first sang on his radio shows, she was known as "Little Dolly." But she "kept growing up and getting bigger." At the age of twelve, then, she was very definitely introduced as Dolly Parton.

Just as she had a clear idea of herself as a singer, Dolly knew how she wanted to look. She bleached her hair a white-blond before she even started high school. And she was beginning to tease it into the bouffant hairstyle that was just becoming popular. Puffed way out on the sides and top, it added a few inches to her height of an even five feet. "I had the biggest hair in school," she says. Now she laughs about it: "When people say that less is more, I say *more* is more. *Less* is *less*. I go for more."

But she also explains that the changes she was making in her appearance "came from a very serious place." Dolly was already a performer. She was beginning to create a stage personality for a *star*.

Her uncle Bill Owens had begun to think his niece *could* be a star. Bill, his brothers Louis and Robert, and Dolly began to rehearse—and rehearse and rehearse, often two or three nights a week. They would start at six in the evening, and play and sing until eleven, or until Dolly was so tired she could hardly keep her eyes open. "I was a brave little soldier," Dolly says of those days. With her uncles backing her up on their guitars, Dolly sang everywhere she could, from covered-dish suppers to gas station openings.

Then Bill Owens managed the almost impossible. The Grand Ole Opry had a policy against letting anyone under eighteen perform. But Uncle Bill got Dolly onstage during a Friday night performance. She sang a song by country star George Jones and had two encores. "It was just more than I could really believe," she says about her premature debut at the Opry.

Bill Owens also went with Dolly all the way to Lake Charles, Louisiana, to make a record. Dolly cut a single for a company called Gold Band Records. On one side was a pop song Dolly had written with Bill called "Puppy Love." On the other side was a mournful country-and-western tune Dolly, Bill, and Louis wrote together—"Girl Left Alone."

When they got back to the Smokies, Bill took the record—and Dolly—around to all the small radio stations. Very few played "Puppy Love." But more important, Dolly says, was that "it was a start, and we had big dreams."

Bill Owens sent tapes of Dolly singing her own songs to Nashville record companies and music publishers. When she was barely fourteen, she was signed up by Buddy Killen of Tree International Publishing Company as a songwriter. And Mr. Killen helped her get a recording contract with Mercury Records. Two months after her sixteenth birthday, Mercury released

Dolly's single "It's Sure Gonna Hurt." The record was heard briefly on some of the Knoxville stations.

While all this was going on, of course, Dolly was still in school. She was an average student, making mostly B-minuses and C-pluses in her classes. She still carried the homemade lunches Avie Lee prepared for all her children—things like cornbread and pork. Dolly marched in the Sevier County High School band, playing snare drums with a shy, red-haired girl named Judy Ogle. Judy had known Dolly since they were

seven. And she was more than just a friend—Judy believed in Dolly's dreams as much as Dolly did.

Dolly had dates, too, like any other teenager. She was talkative, bubbly, very likable—and determined. One of the boys she dated remembers Dolly saying the most important thing in her life was making it as a country singer.

Some of the kids at Sevier County High School still laughed at Dolly's dream of being a star. And some of the teachers there didn't think Dolly sang well enough to appear at school assemblies. They thought her voice was peculiar. And they didn't like country music. As one of Dolly's old classmates explains, "People from the city always looked down on people from the country."

Not that Sevierville was really a city—it had a population of only 3000 people. But Dolly *was* from the country. She joked to a friend at the time, "I live so far back in Sevier County that when you get your bills, they're already past due."

Dolly soon learned not to talk about her records, or her success on the Cas Walker shows. But her critics would get their comeuppance. (Only three years after Dolly graduated, a Sevier County judge would proclaim an annual Dolly Parton Day.)

Dolly single-mindedly worked at her music. And she stayed in school. She was the first person in her family to finish high school.

The day Dolly graduated, she announced to her classmates that she was going to Nashville the next day. Her uncle Bill and his family had moved there a few weeks before. Dolly would stay with them until she could afford a place of her own. And she told everybody that she wouldn't come back until she "made it."

The next day she climbed aboard the Greyhound bus with a cardboard suitcase full of dirty laundry that she hadn't had the time to wash. But she was on her way to Nashville, the "country music capital of the world." It was 1964. Dolly was eighteen years old.

# 3

# Girl Singer

That suitcase full of dirty laundry was to have a long-lasting effect on Dolly's life. Just after she arrived in Nashville on the Greyhound, Dolly took her dirty clothes to the Wishy Washy Laundromat. She stuffed her laundry into an empty machine and poured in some soap. Then she bought a soda and went outside to take a look around.

That's when a good-looking young man drove past in a white 1963 Chevrolet. The young man must have thought Dolly was pretty attractive, too, because he honked his horn and waved. As Dolly says, "Being

from the country, I was real friendly, because everybody in the country knows everybody else." She does admit that she was "maybe flirtin' a little, too."

The young man drove around the block and pulled up at the curb where Dolly was standing. His name was Carl Dean. He was twenty-one years old, tall and dark, and kind of shy. Dolly said later he reminded her a little of her daddy.

Carl asked Dolly for a date. But Dolly felt she couldn't date him until she knew him better. She did tell Carl he could call on her at her uncle's apartment.

When Dolly tells the story of their meeting now, she makes a joke about it: "We met at the Wishy Washy, and it's been wishy-washy ever since." But there was really nothing wishy-washy about Carl Dean. He and Dolly would be married two years later, as soon as he had served in the Army.

And, in the meantime, there was always Dolly's singing career. She was impatient because things weren't happening quickly enough. She told Bud Killen at Tree Publishing that she wanted out of her contract. Then she went to every record company in Nashville. She sang them her songs. And every record company turned her down—except one. That was Monument Records, run by Fred Foster.

For Mr. Foster, Dolly was exactly what he looked for in a singer. She wrote her own music, and she had a very special sound.

Her mother had always said Dolly's voice sounded the way it did because her tonsils had swelled and burst when she was very young. It's more likely that her sound is unusual because Dolly grew up without being influenced by singers on TV or in the movies—the Partons' church allowed neither. And Lee Parton's old radio got such poor reception that even the voices of the stars at the Opry were muffled.

Dolly developed a sound that's all her own—a high, clear soprano. Sometimes it's pure and piercing; sometimes it has a touch of vibrato, a kind of quiver; sometimes it lilts.

"The instant you heard her, you would never forget that was Dolly Parton," Mr. Foster said. Dolly puts it another way: "My voice is strange." She says people have to get used to it. Then they either grow to like it a lot. Or they never like it at all.

As well as having a sound of her own, Dolly was very pretty, with a stunning figure. She had a lot of charm. Also, she reminded Mr. Foster of some of his own relatives—he was from North Carolina.

He signed Dolly to a recording contract. He gave her enough money to find an apartment of her own. And he paid her a small weekly salary, out of which she had to pay her rent, send money home to her family, and eat.

Those were very lean times for Dolly. She says that once, for two weeks, she lived on nothing but hotdog relish and mustard—that was all she had in her refrigerator. "I still can't eat a bit of relish," she says.

And, unfortunately, Mr. Foster wanted Dolly to record pop music. At the time, Dolly was one hundred percent against it. She wanted to sing country music, and only country music. Perhaps she had concentrated so long on becoming a country star that the idea of doing anything else threw her. But she did write more than one hundred songs for Combine, the music-publishing part of Monument Records. And she took part-time jobs, as a waitress, and as a receptionist at a company that made neon signs.

Then, in 1966, one of the songs Dolly had written—"Put It Off Until Tomorrow"—was recorded by a singer named Bill Phillips. Dolly herself sang harmony on the recording. And the single made the country-music Top 10. Many people said the record's success was due to Dolly's unusual voice. Her name wasn't on the label. But disc jockeys who played the record always called attention to the "mystery voice" singing harmony.

Not long after that, Fred Foster agreed to let Dolly cut a country record. They didn't really agree on the *kind* of country song she should sing. Dolly wanted to do a slow ballad. And Mr. Foster wanted her to sing something bouncy. The song they finally chose was called "Dumb Blonde."

The words to the song were corny, saying things

like, "Just because I'm blonde, don't think I'm dumb." But the tune was lively and Dolly soon had a hit on her hands. She followed it with a song she had written herself, "Something Fishy." That, too, was immediately popular.

The country music fan magazines started writing about Dolly. And, pretty soon, everybody was talking about the great new singer. It wasn't long before Dolly got an unexpected phone call from Porter Wagoner.

Porter Wagoner is one of the longest-lasting country stars around. He has been making hit records for over thirty years. Like Dolly, his singing career began on a local radio show in his hometown, in Missouri. On a daily fifteen-minute program, Porter sang country-and-western songs, then told his listeners about the specials at a local butcher shop.

By the time Dolly got to Nashville, Porter had his own television show. It was shown all over the South and the Midwest. And it had forty-five million viewers.

As Dolly said, at that time she had "met a lot of people, but no real big stars." And Porter was a real big star. She imagined he wanted to record one of the songs she had written. When she went to his office, she took her guitar and sang for him. The song she chose was about "everything being beautiful," Porter Wagoner said. He knew if she could write a song like that one, she had to have a "real soul" inside her.

Then he told Dolly why he had called her. Norma Jean, the female vocalist on Porter's show for seven years, was leaving to get married. And he was thinking of replacing her with Dolly. His television show was sponsored by the Chattanooga Medicine Company. The female singer on the show had to be attractive, sound good—and, above all—be warm and sincere. After all, there was patent medicine to be sold: "Black Draught," and "The Wine of Cardui." Porter Wagoner decided that Dolly Parton could do all of those things.

In the summer of 1967, Dolly began to appear on Porter's television show. She would also travel with the show when it went on the road—over two hundred days a year. Someone said, "Aren't you glad you're not married, or you couldn't go." Dolly answered, "Well, I *am* married. And I *am* going." She and Carl Dean had gotten married the year before, when Dolly was twenty and Carl was twenty-three.

Dolly had explained to Carl about her music, that "it wasn't something I did, it was *me*." She said she wouldn't let anything or anyone stand in her way. They wouldn't have the usual kind of marriage. She told Carl, "The bigger I get, the more demands will be made on my time." Carl said he understood. They were married secretly in Georgia on May 30, 1966. When Dolly went on the road with Porter Wagoner and his band, it was the first of many times that Carl Dean has remained behind in Nashville.

As Dolly has said, Porter believed in her when most people didn't. Porter felt Dolly would catch on. And she did. But it was very hard for her in the beginning.

Don Warden, Porter's manager at the time, says, "People were rough. I felt sorry for Dolly. She had a totally different sound. It took some getting used to." When Dolly would walk out on a stage and start to sing, people in the audience would shout, "Where's Norma Jean?" That was to go on for six or eight months. One of the men in the band remembers Dolly leaving the stage in tears.

So Porter and Dolly practiced singing together on the bus that carried the band from one town to the next. They began to sing duets during the show— Dolly usually sang the melody and Porter the tenor harmony. The duets were a good way of getting the audience used to Dolly's voice.

Porter had asked Dolly to leave Fred Foster's Monument Records and sign with RCA, where Porter had a contract. There they recorded two duet albums that did so well, RCA released a single with Dolly singing alone. It was called, "Just Because I'm a Woman." And it, too, was very successful. Porter had been right—introduce Dolly to people as half of a duet, and they'll learn to like her on her own.

Porter's audience liked flashy clothes, too. And his wardrobe was the flashiest. His suits, made by a company called Nudie of Hollywood, were covered with

rhinestones and sequins. Porter's hair was dyed blond and swept up into a puffy pompadour.

Soon Dolly's onstage costumes were as flashy as Porter's: suits that matched his; long dresses with attached capes and stand-up collars that were sequined; long-sleeved blouses with six-inch flyaway cuffs covered with rhinestones. And she started wearing the platinum wigs for which she has become famous. Dolly was beginning to look like the fairy-tale kings and queens she had admired as a child. And she and the audience loved it. "The glitter is a gimmick," she would say later, "fun for the audience and fun for me, something we can share together. . . . If people think I'm a dumb blond because of the way I look, then they're dumber than they think *I* am." She had always said when she had the money for wigs and fancy clothes and outrageous jewelry, "I'm gonna pile it all over me." And now Dolly had the money. She was making $60,000 a year.

Porter and Dolly won the Country Music Association's Vocal Group of the Year Award in 1968, its Vocal Duo of the Year Award in 1970 and 1971. On top of that, Dolly was to have eleven number-one hit singles while she was working with Porter.

But as successful as she was, Dolly was still Porter Wagoner's "girl singer." It's true that she was now a member of the Grand Ole Opry, just as she had dreamed of being. With Bill Owens, she even owned a music publishing company, Owepar. The "Owe" was for her uncle Bill. The "Par," of course, was for herself. But Dolly wanted to be a real star. And she felt she wasn't going to be a real star as long as she was working for Porter.

Dolly and Porter had their biggest disagreements in the recording studio. Yes, they *had* made many hit records together. But Dolly wanted to try new things. And Porter didn't. Dolly said it took away all the "joy of recording the songs." She was beginning to want to record in a way that would reach a wider audience— not just country-and-western fans.

Porter's answer: "Dolly Parton's career up until she left me was done my way. Had we done the songs she would have liked to have done, the way she would have liked to have done them, it would not have worked. I signed the checks at the time, so we did things my way."

Porter felt many of Dolly's ideas would not be right for his audience. Dolly felt that her songs were "taking somebody else's personality." A musician friend of Dolly's says that was the main reason she left. She wasn't able to "express her music the way she wanted to."

But some of the music people in Nashville said staying with Porter any longer than she did was not part of Dolly's career plan. They felt that Porter Wagoner was a stepping stone, like Bud Killen at Tree

Publishing, and Fred Foster at Monument—that Dolly wouldn't deliberately hurt anyone by stepping *on* him to get where she was going. But she might step *around* somebody if necessary.

Porter didn't want to believe that Dolly was really going to leave the show. Dolly said it was very hard. They had worked together a long time. They had laughed together and cried together. It was hard to split up. But she also said, "You have to dream your own dreams."

At a press conference they held in February of 1974, they announced that they would be going their own ways. Dolly said that Porter "took a little country girl and made something out of her." Maybe only Dolly realized how much farther she could go.

# 4

# Big Plans

In July of that year, Dolly told a reporter that now she felt like a star: she had her own bus for traveling to concert dates. It was beige and white, with a purple stripe. A butterfly was painted on the back. Dolly's single, "Love Is Like a Butterfly," was number one at that time. And she had loved bright-colored butterflies since she was a child.

Inside the bus was a lounge; a complete stereo tape system; Dolly's room, with a bathroom, a fold-out couch, a wig cabinet, and three closets; and bunks and another bathroom for Dolly's musicians. Dolly was

going on the road, looking for that wider audience.

Dolly's family ties were very important to her. She had always dreamed of having a "family show." So she was calling her band the "Traveling Family Band." Its members included her younger brother Randy on bass, two cousins—one on drums, one on steel guitar—and a nonrelative on lead guitar. Later her brother Floyd and sisters Frieda and Rachel joined the band, too. Her younger brothers and sisters had always wanted a family show, Dolly said. Now she had given them one.

Dolly was making her own decisions. And things started out well. In 1975 Dolly won the Country Music Association's Female Vocalist of the Year award. *Cash Box*, *Record World*, and *Billboard* magazines named her the Top Female Vocalist. And *Billboard* also named her the Best Female Singles Artist and Best Songwriter: Female.

Dolly signed a contract to do a television show much like Porter Wagoner's. The show would be called *Dolly!*, and it would be based in Nashville. But Dolly wanted the show to appeal to people in big cities like

New York and Los Angeles, as well as in small towns. So the guests scheduled to appear on the show weren't just country-and-western singers. There were also performers like Marilyn McCoo and Billy Davis, Jr., Anson Williams, Rod McKuen, Emmylou Harris, and Linda Ronstadt.

Emmylou Harris had started out as a folk singer. Now she was singing rock and country as well. Recently she had recorded Dolly's song, "Coat of Many Colors." She was so impressed with the spunkiness of the child in the song that she wanted to meet Dolly. They liked each other immediately.

At about the same time, Dolly met Linda Ronstadt. She, too, had recorded one of Dolly's songs, "I Will Always Love You." Dolly visited Linda and Emmylou in California that year. And they became two of Dolly's biggest promoters. Dolly was to say later, "They have done more for me, as far as their audience, their following, as far as talkin' me up. I'm always jokin' with 'em that I should put 'em on salary for publicity."

Then, in 1976, things started to go wrong. Dolly began to have serious throat problems. Because Dolly's voice is so high, she tends to strain it. She had been singing about 120 concerts a year since she took her band on the road. Lots of those concerts were in small towns, with poor public address systems. Dolly sometimes had to scream to make herself heard over the band.

She had tired herself out. In addition to the concerts, she was taping the television show. And she was traveling back and forth to concerts as far away as Alaska, Hawaii, and Europe. (She had just been named "Top Female Vocalist" in England.)

Her television show wasn't working. Most people—including Dolly herself—thought it just wasn't Dolly. The show's producers had her singing songs she didn't feel comfortable with—old movie tunes, like "Singin' in the Rain." And when country singer Marty Robbins tuned in to the show, he found Dolly singing to a *monkey*. "That made me so mad—Dolly playing second fiddle to a monkey," he says, "that I turned it off. That's not Dolly Parton!"

The Traveling Family Band wasn't working out, either. It wasn't really good enough for Dolly. When she sang in places like the Felt Forum in New York City, reviewers raved about Dolly. But they said her band was weak.

Dolly was beginning to want more than just a country band. Country music, she said, had a simpler sound. It leaned heavily on steel guitars or fiddles. Pop music used horns, strings—the sound was softer and fuller. And Dolly was ready to take a full step away from country-and-western. She said she didn't want her music to be "labeled" anymore. "I'd like my music to be known just as Dolly Parton's music," she said.

Finally, in May 1976, Dolly cancelled all of her

appearances until October. She told the Traveling Family Band that they would regroup in six months. She probably believed it at the time. Dolly said she wanted to get her business straight, and her health back.

Rumors began to fly: that Dolly had had a nervous breakdown, that she was seriously ill, that she was going to die. Actually, Dolly was exhausted. And she was having trouble with her throat. She had nodes—small growths—on her vocal cords. Nodes can lead to permanent hoarseness and even loss of voice control. She had to rest her voice until the nodes shrank. But Dolly was also beginning to think that her career wasn't going where it should be going.

First, Dolly and Carl Dean went on a second honeymoon to Yellowstone National Park. As she described it later, they had a great time. They camped out, and Dolly "unraveled all the wigs, and the high heels, and the makeup."

Next, she and Carl took all Dolly's nieces and nephews to Disney World. Then Dolly flew to New York to talk to the people at RCA about changing her sound. Dolly wanted to be a "crossover" singer—one who could cross the line between country-and-western and popular music. She got RCA's full support.

Dolly also wanted to find a manager of her own. When she was younger, her uncle Bill had been a kind of manager. Next she had used Porter's manager, then

her uncle Louis. Now she wanted a manager who could dream as big as she did. She wanted a manager who knew the right people, who could make her a superstar. She chose the Los Angeles firm of Katz-Gallin-Cleary, an agency that represented Cher, the Osmonds, and Olivia Newton-John.

Dolly said she chose Katz-Gallin because they had connections in network television and knew movie producers. But perhaps the real reason was, "They make me look important because they make me feel important. I have a need to be important." That's what Dolly told a magazine writer at the time.

The people at Katz-Gallin helped Dolly put together another band—the Traveling Family Band was a thing of the past. Dolly called the new band "Gypsy Fever." The musicians were "from everyplace, really." But they weren't from Nashville. And a lot of the music people in Nashville were beginning to say Dolly thought Nashville and country music weren't good enough for her. They also said Dolly had faked her illness to get out of singing at her scheduled country-and-western concerts.

That made Dolly very angry. She said the doctor had told her, "If you sing, and if you strain those nodes, it'll do permanent damage." But even more upsetting to her was the gossip about why she fired her first band. Some people said she did it because she felt her family was *beneath* her.

Dolly said it almost broke her heart to tell them she had decided to make some changes. But "they understood, as much as anybody could."

Perhaps Dolly explained it best when she said, "I had big plans and big dreams. . . . Every country girl wants to go to the city."

# 5

# Movie Star, Superstar

Dolly was tasting her freedom. On her first album with "Gypsy Fever," *New Harvest . . . First Gathering,* she sang a little of everything: rock, folk, a ballad, soul, an inspirational song—and, of course, country. As Dolly said, "I don't want to leave country. I want to take it with me wherever I go."

She had made the right moves. Her band was good. Her first album with them was something to be proud of. "It was the first time in my whole life I got to do something totally on my own," Dolly said about *New Harvest.* "It's one of the greatest thrills in my life."

Dolly had indeed "crossed over," from country to just about everything. What was she going to do next?

Her management company saw to it that Dolly appeared on *The Tonight Show* with Johnny Carson. She enjoyed herself and was invited back right away. As Dolly put it, "Katz-Gallin got me on the show. But *Johnny* asked me back." Clearly, Mr. Carson was charmed by Dolly, as were his millions of viewers. After her second appearance, NBC reported a tremendous amount of mail about Dolly.

Dolly and her band went on a three-week tour with Mac Davis, another crossover country singer. She sang "Coat of Many Colors" on Mac's television special and two other songs she had written in a duet with Mac.

Then, in April 1977, Dolly took her band on the road: Los Angeles, San Francisco, Denver, Chicago, New York. She attracted huge crowds sprinkled with celebrities like Mick Jagger, Bette Midler, Candice Bergen, Bruce Springsteen, Barbra Streisand. One reporter wrote, "It was gush at first sight." Another— in New York City—noted, "The packed crowd cheered on Miss Parton . . . from the moment she swept onto the stage." Dolly was a Star with a capital *S*.

And then? Dolly flew to the British Isles, where she met "a real live queen"—Queen Elizabeth II. And the queen told Dolly she had enjoyed her show.

Dolly's next album, *Here You Come Again,* outsold

in *two weeks* any of her other albums. It would eventually go platinum, which means one million albums sold. At the end of the year, Dolly was interviewed by Barbara Walters on her ABC special. When Barbara asked Dolly to turn her own life into a fairy tale, Dolly began with, "She lived in a small town in the mountains . . . which she loved, because it was a comfort, because she knew there was love and security there, in her family." And she ended with, "So she worked hard and she dreamed a lot. And one day it came true. She was a fairy princess and she lived happily ever after. . . ."

Now, Dolly said, she wanted to "do TV, some specials, and I want to write some movies." Did she want to act in a movie? She said she hadn't thought about it.

But other people had. One reporter who knew Dolly well in Nashville said, "Most of the other women in country music are limited to singing and writing. But I think Dolly could run a show business empire. Dolly in the movies? Heck, yeah!"

Somebody else thought so, too—Jane Fonda. In fact, once Ms. Fonda had come up with the idea of making a comedy about secretaries, she knew Dolly *had* to be in it. She wasn't worried about the fact that Dolly hadn't acted before. Ms. Fonda said, "Anyone who can write 'Coat of Many Colors,' and sing it the way she does, can do anything."

The movie would be called *Nine to Five*. Dolly's character in the movie was based, Jane Fonda says, on "who Dolly is and what she seems like"—an incredible-looking, not-at-all-dumb blond. When Dolly saw the script, she knew she would do the movie.

"It was so funny," she said later, "because I didn't know exactly what the movies were all about. I just assumed they would start in the front and follow the story to keep up the excitement." So Dolly memorized the whole script—not just her part, but Lily Tomlin's part, Jane Fonda's part, everybody's part.

Dolly said she got a "kick out of it later, when [she] saw how few lines they do a day, and how they shoot out of sequence."

How was Dolly as an actress? Lily Tomlin said, "She was wonderful! She's so quick, so natural, so dazzling, down-to-earth, bigger than life. You could have replaced Jane or me in a more satisfactory way. But once you got the idea for Dolly to be in *her* role, it would have been more of a disappointment without her."

The title song that Dolly wrote for *Nine to Five* was

nominated for an Academy Award. And it went to the top of both the pop and country charts. Eventually, it sold over a million copies as a single.

About her acting Dolly said, "There were places I thought I was real good. But there were also places I was real average and places where I was yuck." But audiences—and film reviewers—loved her. Many people feel Dolly was the main reason the movie brought in 120 million dollars.

The year *Nine to Five* was released, Dolly won a "People's Choice" award. And her music wasn't forgotten—she also won a Female Vocalist of the Year from the Academy of Country Music. Dolly was thirty-four years old.

Dolly said then, "I knew if my career went the way I wanted it to, Vegas, the movies, and all that stuff would eventually come."

And it has. Of her movie *Rhinestone,* with Sylvester Stallone, a reporter wrote: "The best thing in *Rhinestone* is Dolly Parton, who seems to be able to survive just about any movie unscathed." Universal Pictures is working on a multimillion-dollar deal with Dolly's production company—they want Dolly to star in more films.

Dolly continues to sing—she has had her own show in Las Vegas, along with some television specials. And her duet with Kenny Rogers, "Islands in the Stream," was the best-selling single in 1983.

Her songwriting hasn't slowed down, either. Dolly says if she had to give up performing, "it wouldn't bother me too much. But I couldn't live without my writing."

She never knows when she's going to be in a "writing mood." If she has an idea and can't write it down immediately, she says she "can't even carry on a halfway decent conversation."

Dolly gets what she calls "looking headaches," headaches from "being so aware of everything around me," Dolly explains. "I don't want to miss a thing."

She wrote all the songs for *Rhinestone*—close to twenty of them—in a little over three weeks. That doesn't come close to her record, though, twenty songs in a little over twenty-four hours—she wrote from three in the afternoon straight through to the following evening.

Dolly owns a house in Hawaii on the island of Oahu, and an apartment in New York City. But she hasn't given up Nashville. She also owns a twenty-three-room mansion on a farm just outside the city limits. That's where her husband, Carl Dean, spends most of his time.

As Dolly explains it, Carl is a loner. When they married, Carl accepted the fact that Dolly's music was her life. And Dolly says she accepted the fact that Carl did not want to be a part of her career. For a time he worked in the paving business with his father. Now he takes care of the Tennessee farm.

Dolly says of Carl, "He's the man God intended me to have. Mind you, I'd be the first to admit ours is the weirdest relationship. I mean, who else but us could spend so much time apart and still make it work? I reckon a good part of the reason is that he's just the funniest man I've ever known. I can't imagine my life without him." But she also says, "I don't really want to be with him all the time. And he don't want to be with me all the time. He likes his freedom."

Things have changed since Dolly was a little girl who climbed trees to sing so she could pretend that she was on stage. She is very rich. She even has a bodyguard. But has she lost her country roots?

Not at all, she says. "You can offer me any amount of money . . . if it don't feel right, I don't want it. That comes from that down-home Tennessee feeling of knowing what's right and what's real." When Dolly talks of country people—which means herself—she praises their earth sense, their common sense. And she says she wouldn't trade it for anything else in the world.

Dolly's old friend Judy Ogle is now her secretary. And Dolly and her family remain very close. Dolly's parents are proud, independent people. She bought them a farm outside Nashville: "Daddy gets antsy if he's anywhere around where he can hear autos," she

says. But she gives her mother a new car every year. And Dolly says she still would "rather die than do anything to hurt or embarrass Mama or Daddy."

Dolly has no regrets. She says she's had some disappointments. "Any time you put out a record or a movie, you hope it's gonna be a hit. I give it everything I got when I'm doin' it, and then I go on to somethin' else." When she's asked about the pressures of being a star, she says, "I like being famous. I wanted to be famous."

Dolly says that if she were a waitress, she'd end up owning the restaurant. If she were a barmaid, she'd make everybody happy, tell the worst jokes, lend everybody money. "Being a star," Dolly says, "just means that you find your own special place and that you shine where you are."

And that's what Dolly Parton has always done best.